By Scott Peterson
Illustrations by Mike Parobeck, Rick Burchett,
and Don Desclos

A GOLDEN BOOK • NEW YORK
Golden Books Publishing Company, Inc., Racine, Wisconsin 53404

 Library of Congress Catalog Card Number: 95-75353 ISBN: 0-307-10007-3 MCMXCVII

Bruce Wayne was a happy little boy. He had everything. He lived with his parents in a beautiful house in Gotham City. His friend Alfred the butler lived with him, too.

Then one night a robber attacked Bruce's mother and father. Now Bruce's safe, happy world had changed. Alfred tried to reassure the boy, but he never felt the same again.

Bruce decided to spend the rest of his life fighting crime. As he grew up, he traveled the world to learn everything he could about it.

Bruce Wayne went to the Far East and studied martial arts with the greatest masters. He practiced and practiced, turning his body into the ultimate fighting machine.

Bruce developed his mind, too. He studied science with the most brilliant professors. He studied police work with the best detectives. Now he would be able to track down criminals and solve crimes.

After several years, Bruce returned to Gotham City. He had a plan. Far beneath Wayne Manor was a cave that only he and Alfred knew about.

The cave became Bruce's secret headquarters. There he put everything he would need to help him fight crime: computers, books, and a laboratory. He also installed a gym to keep his body superstrong.

Bruce built the most amazing car in the world. It was bulletproof and superfast. And he could even control the car by using his computers.

Bruce was ready to fight crime—but he didn't know how to begin.

Then one day a bat crashed through his window. It gave him an idea. "Bats scare people," Bruce thought. "I'll be like a bat, and criminals will fear me!"

And that's how Bruce Wayne became . . . Batman!

Soon Batman made friends with Commissioner Gordon, head of the Gotham City Police. Whenever there was trouble, the Commissioner called Batman with the Bat-Signal—a superpowerful spotlight.

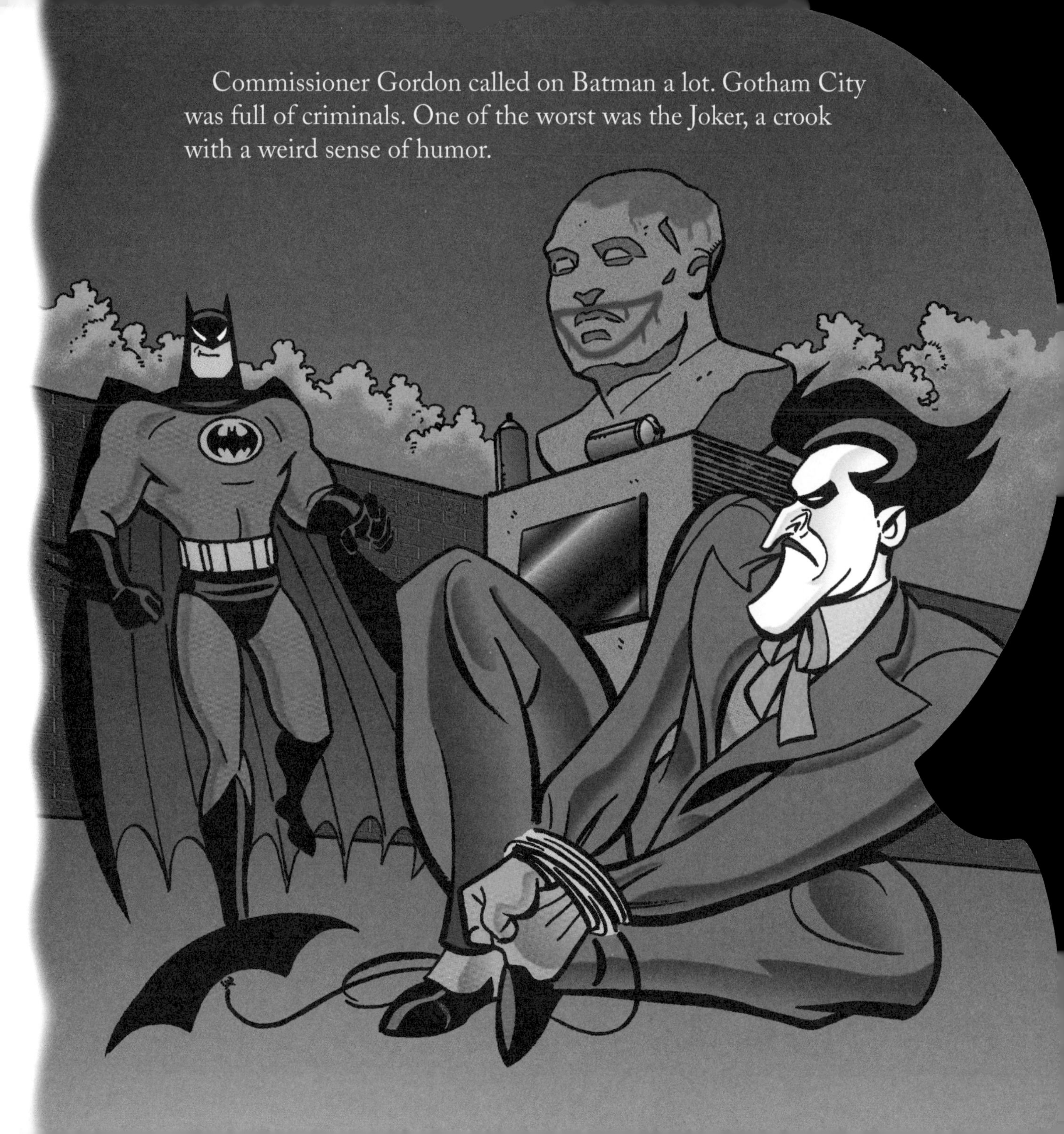

Commissioner Gordon called on Batman a lot. Gotham City was full of criminals. One of the worst was the Joker, a crook with a weird sense of humor.

Another clever criminal was Catwoman, a talented jewel thief.

Batman battled the Penguin, a big-time robber who used birds and umbrellas in his plots . . .

He also fought Two-Face, a troublemaker who did everything in twos . . .

and the Riddler, who tried to confuse Batman with puzzle-filled crimes!

But Batman, the greatest crime-fighter of all time, will always win in the end.

SPOTLIGHT ON BATMAN

SECRET IDENTITY: Bruce Wayne

ALIAS: The Dark Knight

OCCUPATION: No known profession; multimillionaire

KNOWN RELATIVES: Thomas and Martha Wayne (parents, deceased)

BASE OF OPERATIONS: Gotham City, U.S.A.

HEIGHT: 6 feet 2 inches

WEIGHT: 210 pounds

EYES: Blue

HAIR: Black

POWERS AND WEAPONS: A martial-arts expert and brilliant detective, Batman is Gotham City's master crime-fighter. He plans his battles against criminals from the Batcave, his underground headquarters. Batman drives his shiny, super-powered Batmobile into action and always wears his utility belt, which carries lasers, gas pellets, silk ropes, and a Batarang.